CUPID'S
Bow

CUPID'S
Bow

ASHLEY E. CLYKE

authorHOUSE®

AuthorHouse™
1663 Liberty Drive
Bloomington, IN 47403
www.authorhouse.com
Phone: 1 (800) 839-8640

Published by AuthorHouse   07/08/2015

ISBN: 978-1-5049-2234-0 (sc)
ISBN: 978-1-5049-2233-3 (e)

Library of Congress Control Number: 2015911085

Print information available on the last page.

PINK SATIN SHEETS

In the chamber
in the shadows and candlelight
Pink Satin Sheets
move as flames
dance round
us indulging in -delight

Delight as known by us two
tumbling in the satin
doing things we shouldn't do

You laugh
as I kiss you
you Scream
when I sigh
You pursue
you don't have to
come to me-

aye. aye. aye.

CONNECT

We connect
like we're free
There's more to
love
This Love
than sexdreams
It's deep in my eyes
I see it in yours
-this power struggle
this echoing silent roar.
We're fighting-us
Closing doors.
shoving to get away,
playing 'cause we're torn.
Lost and looking, searching
-Dividing
Using this physical
Relationship
To buy time
'cause we're hiding.

I need you by now,
You've been here too long
I gave you my heart.
And babe I know I'm not wrong.

MY WAY

You know,
being with you makes me
think.
Why are we never alone?
I think you're shy.
You are always being
the proper guy.

I'm not so genteel;
I'm naughty when I'm real.

I can give you a thrill,
push you past
release, until …
Well, never mind;
not a lot of men
can handle my kind.
Caught your eye.
Is it interest
that I spy?
A smile like that
can leave a girl
mesmerized.
Well, time to go home.
Don't worry;
I won't roam.

What?
You want me to stay?
Oh, you nasty boy.
I thought you would see things my way.

AFTERLUST

Slow pull

on a cigarette.

Smoke drifting.

Clouds forming.

Tension pulsing.

Us in bed;

the afterlust

clears

my

head.

HEE-HEE

I'm new here; will you show me
Around? You foreign,
Exciting new friend
I've found,
I don't speak the language,
But I understand you.
Interesting.
You're understanding me too.
I love
What I've seen.
I had fun; you did too.
It's not over yet?
I should still follow you?
Such a nice place to eat;
This wine and that tune.
Come back to your house?
You're being naughty,
Aren't you?
I'm not sure
I should.
But nothing fun
Happens to me,
So
You show the way,
And I'll follow.
Hee-hee.

WHAT WOULD YOU DO?

I saw you down the hall.
I know your number;
I should call.
But what would you say?
"Come over."
And would I stay?

If I knock on your door,
Would you invite me in?
Should I give up to chance
That we might spend the night
In carnal sin?

Awkward seduction
The look in my eye.
Would you sense it?
Would you answer my cry?
Would you feel
The thick layer
Of sweat on my skin?
Would you taste the exotic spice

That flavors my lips?
Would you take your hands
down
over
and past
the curve of my hips?

Bend me over.
And would you make a move?

Rip off my clothes.
What would you do?

By The Water

By the water
Leaf and Grass
A silhouette
-your slender figure's
lines are cast

chaste

innocent

-Virginal,

my timid soul endeavors to ask
yet in your presence
a coward I am, and flown is the chance.
Please
Allow to me
High Natures Prize
Your Love
Your Beauty
and the courage I can't find.

Gentle Love

gentle lover
gentle, man
pleasing touch
caring hand
gently hard, gently firm
fixed and steady
strong and learned
true
seduction
soft
delay
temperate
love
don't go—
remain.

SEX

Sex—
What you want,
What you get.

Sex—
Reason why?
'Cause we met.

Sex—
Sex can be
Deliberate.

Sex—
Flavors life—
And it ain't over yet.

Sex!

BLACK

lost in Black.
Black
silky fleece-
I've lost myself.

in torrents
completely-

In such that
I can not hide.

Exquisite the feeling

touching your body
kissing,
reeling,
… never before
am I found?
it's deceiving.
Persuasive you are,
and to this fleece you did lead me
Black fleece
through which you can see me.

You Sow What You Reap

You said good-bye
For the tenth time.
But
You come back;
Then
You leave.

I use you too,
As well.

We are entwined in a passionate
Spell.

Hard, soft, sweet—
You treat me like a piece of
Meat.

But I have my revenge.
Ignore me; you'll see
I'm what you need.
Remember, dear lover-
You sow what you reap.

WOULD YOU? WHY NOT?

"You know what?
I just noticed,
You're my type
You are actually very
Hot."

"would you with me?"

Why

Why not?

Should we

Could we?

Can we

Would we?

I wouldn't mind.

Let's give it a try…

Okay.

I can't believe
this is how
We
Decide.

HONEY

Golden honey
has us
For Used Instead of Oil.
-the sword and the sheath
would have spoiled.

Sticky golden syrup
Smack Smack
Pleasuring what's yours
And mine
-and in this honey
We are stuck in a love
Trap.

Yet, honey is not
used for this.
BUT for my sword
and for your sheath-
To explain what I mean

Honey
Is the
State
Of lust
That sword and sheath
Must have. They must.

DO YOU CARE TO
DANCE WITH ME

I hear a song
When we're together
It's sweet,
I'm listening.
But so far we just sit together
And don't do
Anything.

I'm going to
Take a chance
And ask
Please answer honestly,
On my bed I love to dance
Do you care to dance with me?

RIPE

I want you
Now,
So
I'll get your attention
Ready for this?
Here's a bold suggestion:

Ripe am I.

Pick me.Pluck.
I'm Good for your Digestion.

THOSE

Those
Private
Sexy
Pleasures.
Kept in,
Secret
Black
Intimate-
,places that renders.
When
Lace that comes
undone
-with
Lust
That does
Engulf and succumb
Reveals
That
What was pure
And enjoys
That what has
Become.

ROCK HARD

You're
Rock hard,
Stiff and stern.
Just smack me,
Babe—teach;
I'll learn.

Saddle up!
Rough and tough.
Bronco ride.
Search my stuff.

Rugged, bold,
Hot and cold.
In a master's place
And in control.

NATURALLY

Follow me.
Let's shake the trees
Get lost
in the
undergrowth.
be naked and free
I feel the need
To do the deed
like Animals
Mating,
Doing it
Naturally.

WHAT DO YOU MEAN

"But, what do you mean?"

Racy, raunchy, dirty, down-low, and *wet*. Hands in butter. Chicken *breast*. Oil springs—a *mattress*. Overwhelming *musky scent*. Sweat, a ride—stopping— *spent*. A tug. A grip. *Condi*ments. Salt and pepper— add some spice. Mix the paint, *blow* on dice—jackpot round! *Horn* makes sound. Giddyup, horse to mound.

"Get it?"

HUMAN BODY

the
Human body?
-we have them,
Right?
Excellent!
You are bright.
and what
are they
for?
Come now
You must know of
Some more.
Of What is
Their Purpose?
What potential
They have stored?
The service they
Provide ?
Well now,
Of course you must know
There are
Male and female
And low and behold
one
Is
Like a glove.
And the other
Has
A tail.

Put them together
And what do they
share ? – Love

Right.

Yes my beautiful
Who is as keen as a dove
Let me demonstrate
And we will make love!

HEY, GIRL

Mmm, I'm so
Horny.

Hey, girl—look at that man!
That man's so hot,
when he writes a check,
the watermarks get
wet.

Lay it on me, sugar!
That's it; I see you looking
at me.
You want some of this?
It's EASY
You just come over here now.

I'll give it to you;
I'll give it to you good!

I ain't lying!

You know you want some of this.
Everyone wants some of this.
I want some of this.

Look at you laughing.
Come back!
Come back here.

How are we going to
get together if
you're leaving!?

Damn, girl.

I'm sure that
was my soul mate
who just walked
by.

Why you laughing?

You shouldn't be laughing at me.
I'm going to marry that man someday.

Laughing at me
Like you could do any better.

You couldn't pick up a man
if you were the last free taxicab
at an airport.

Ha!

THE SEAMAN SAID

A stormy
Night
In a drinking hole.

Near the harbor,
The truth unfolds.

The seaman said,
With a glint in his eye,
"Listen, dearie, this is why.
Because
I can kiss you,
Tease you,
And
Leave you.

Friends with benefits—
I can even retrieve you.

This is my right.

Love's too much for reason."

I want a life that's
Colored, like seasons,

Where I do what I want,
Say what I please,
Arrive and depart,
Sail on the breeze.

There was a ship
With crewmen free.
They visited every port
Because they sail the seven seas.

As The Flower Petals Fly

As the flower petals fly,
Yield like a branch of the cherry blossom tree,
I
Am
The wind
That pollinates, bringing you
Your seed.

Yield until
The
Petals
Dance and fly because of me.

MOLDING CLAY

Form,
Take shape,
Become, and obey.
Give.
Make ready.
Be my molding clay.

DO IT TO ME

Do it to me.
Do it to me.

Do it to me good.
Do it as I imagine.
Set fire to the wood.
Crude, sticky sap,
Smoke in a smothering flame.
Do it to me.
Do it to me.
Fire.
Blaze! Blaze! Blaze!

You Pirate

On a ship
At sea,
I am captive.
You captivate me.
Approach me,
Touch me,
Be private.
My treasures
Are
Hidden.
Undress me,
Ravage me,
Take me prisoner,
You
Pirate.

TRY

Now closer
Come hither.
You know I can see right through you.
-Thinking of how now to seduce me?
Why not? it is a good idea.
Test me, if you do it wouldn't hurt.
You're Thirsty.
I'm Quenching.
Try, I'm tempting

Here I am
Right before you
READ MY MIND

, I've tequila at home
a key to my
room

Don't be shy Sexy Lover
If you knew the things I'd do to you.

In The Place

In the place that hides my secrets, you taste my
treasures for
private reasons,
Gently, your touch leaves me in pleasure, have
my body
raw
Intense.
Release-
release me,

That's better.

How You Do Trust Me

How you do trust me,
Eat from my hand.
Closer, I approach.
Touch me, kiss.
Beautiful.
We're man and woman.

OPEN

Hey, Sexy.
Open.
Let me inside
You've been swimming
'round
The fishbowl
Of
My mind.
I'll be fish feed.
You
Nibble a bit
And after your
Hooked.
I'll let you have
It.

Now

Now,
Here's my number.
I know you won't
Call.
But
When you want sex,
I'll
Look better—
That's all.

Secret Meat

Oh, I can!
I'm delish
Sex with me
A gourmet dish.

I'll serve you
Up
Drink you
From a Styrofoam
Cup.
Fries and gravy
Dip, Repeat.
Get your hands dirty
When you
Eat
Smother you
With so much sauce
You'll fly like a
Side salad
That you
Toss.
Too much sweet
A tasty treat
Chocolate, Cheese
And
Secret meat.

PANTS

Pants
You should be my pants
No,
You should be in my pants-
Like you're pants.
Like you're tight,
Close fitting
Pants.
The kind of pants
That
Rides up and makes you
Uncomfortable
Pants
The kind that
Gets in between
The places that are
Personal and pleasurable
Pants.
Maybe even
Coveralls.
But definitely
Pants.

LUCKY

"We'll get in trouble,"
You whisper back
When I say, "Let's do it in the bathroom."

You're so timid!
And I like that;
When I'm with you, the world seems to relax.

I spend time
Thinking,
And you know what I find?

That I'm the luckiest person.

With you I'm alive.

OWN ME

Love,
You sexy beast,
You thought that
You owned me,
But I'm still
Wild and free.
Try
Try to attain,
Try to possess
The minx that you see;
You can acquire
But never own in confidence.

ENCHANTING

Enchanting,
The part where
She kisses him
And they tumble
Onto the bed,
His hand beneath
Her head,
Her lips pressed
Against his'
When he lifts up
Her dress
And enters,
Aware of nothing
But her heaving
Bosom
And the fire
In her
That he must
Put to rest.

ONLY YOU

I love you so, and I am caught.
Caught!
With no ability to manage escape—
Because of you.
Only you;
Everything is all of you

That charges this
Pulsing rhythm
That races from out
My heart.
In this hole,
This well, this water bucket
I sit in,
Submerged in blissful insanity.

Printed in the United States
By Bookmasters